Farmer Ham Too

Written by
Alec Sillifant

Illustrated by
Mike Spoor

The crows were unhappy,

and they were unhappy because, as usual,

they were moping around in a muddy field of sprouts.

All day long they would sit in the muddy
field of sprouts, dreaming of their old cornfield.

"I think I'm sprouting
green feathers,"
one crow sighed.

"That's nothing," moaned another.
"I'm going sprout of my mind."

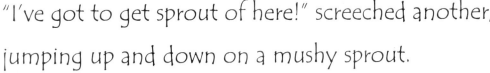

"I've got to get sprout of here!" screeched another,
jumping up and down on a mushy sprout.

"Why don't you?" said a stranger,
sitting on the fence.
"Just over the hill is a field
full of plump, juicy, golden corn."

"But a great big monster guards it," shouted all the crows at once.

"Does it really?" said the stranger.

"Follow me…"

…And off he flew.

The stranger landed on the shoulder of the scarecrow in Farmer Ham's cornfield but the rest of the crows were too scared to do the same.

"There's nothing to be frightened of," he said, pecking the scarecrow's head. "It's just a big, ugly doll."

All the crows looked at each other, grinned and started shouting, **"Silly old Farmer Ham!"**

Farmer Ham had just finished ploughing
his potato field when he noticed
what was happening in his cornfield.

One of the crows saw him and said, "Look who it is!"

"Should we leave him any corn?" said another.

"Yeah," said a third. "The one on his big toe!"

All the crows laughed, shouting, "Silly old Farmer Ham!"

The next day, Farmer Ham was up very early
and, as all the crows watched him, he walked
into his cornfield and picked up the scarecrow.

"Do you think the scarecrow is ill?" said one of the crows.
"Well, he has been under the weather," said another.

Farmer Ham walked out of the cornfield
and into his barn as all the crows
laughed, shouting,
"Silly old Farmer Ham!"

On the third day, the crows were still in the cornfield
when Farmer Ham went to his vegetable patch
and picked a huge, round pumpkin.

"Do you think he's going to make a salad with that?" said one of the crows.

"I don't know," said another. "But I'm sure he'll lettuce know."

All the crows laughed, shouting,

"Silly old Farmer Ham!"

On the fourth day,
Farmer Ham went into his
barn and came out carrying a bag.
In it was a twisted top hat, a slimy scarf, a dirty
old boot, a tatty jacket and a ripped pair of trousers.

"Looks like Farmer Ham has sacked the scarecrow," said one crow.

"It's not surprising," said another. "He wasn't outstanding in his field!"

All the crows laughed and ate corn, shouting,

"Silly old Farmer Ham!"

As the sun rose over the hill and the crows woke up, the scarecrow was back in the cornfield once again.

"As if we'd ever be scared by that big, ugly, doll a second time," said a crow.

The stranger jumped up onto the scarecrow's shoulder. "It looks even uglier than I remember," he said.

All the crows laughed, shouting,

"Silly old Farmer Ha

Slowly the scarecrow's head turned
and looked at the crows.
The crows looked back wide-eyed
and open-beaked with terror,

as the scarecrow shouted...

"BO

Farmer Ham watched as all the terrified crows flew off, desperate to get as far away as possible from the 'monster' in the cornfield. When he was sure they had all gone, he carefully took the hollowed out pumpkin off his head and smiled.

This one's for you, Beth.
M.S.

For Alison, Sarah, Simon, Rupert, and Mark,
without all of whom none of this would have been
possible – so blame them.
A.S.

First published in 2005
by Meadowside Children's Books
185 Fleet Street London EC4A 2HS

Text © Alec Sillifant 2005
Illustrations © Mike Spoor 2005
The rights of Alec Sillifant and Mike Spoor
to be identified as the author and illustrator
have been asserted by them in accordance with
the Copyright, Designs and Patents Act, 1988.

A CIP catalogue record for this book
is available from the British Library.
10 9 8 7 6 5 4 3 2 1
Printed in U.A.E.